Dedicated to children who like myself grow up wearing hand-me-down clothes and to all parents and grandparents who teach us the value of sharing.

- Deborah L. Delaronde

Dedicated to my daughter Kristen who I used as the model for Flora in this story.

- Gary Chartrand

Special thanks to Robin Hood Multifoods for their support and legal permission in using their 1940-50's company flour sack and logo within the story. Robin Hood Multifoods was incorporated in 1909 and operated their first mill in Moose Jaw, Saskatchewan.

Also, special thanks to Five Roses Flour company for their support and legal permission in using their 1926 company flour sack and logo within the story. the first mill was in operation in 1881 in Winnipeg, Manitoba, 1886 in Montreal, Quebec and 1913 in Medicine Hat, Alberta. In 1915, the first Five Roses cook book was published, the cook book was in daily use in nearly 600,000 Canadian homes.

Going shopping was a big event for Flora's family
who lived in a Metis community a long way from the nearest town.

Before that day arrived, family and friends would bring their shopping lists to
Flora's mom and dad. Flora wanted more than anything in the whole world to be
able to go to town. She wanted to see what towns looked like,
the people who lived there and all the things that were sold in the stores.

Flour Sack Flora

Written by Deborah L. Delaronde

Illustrated by Gary Chartrand

Flora's mom was busy writing her own shopping list.
Flora decided to ask, "Mom, do you think I could go to town with you and dad?"

Flora's mom shook her head, "I'm sorry, Flora. You would need a pretty dress to wear and we can't afford to buy you one." she said.

"At least not this time," she added, wishing more than anything to see Flora without the usual faded and worn jeans.

Flora had a great idea about a dress and went to visit her Grandmother.
Flora found her at the clothes line unclipping and folding flour sack cloths.

"Hi Grandma. Do you have an old dress that you don't want anymore?" she asked.

"Why would you want one of my old dresses?" Grandma asked looking surprised.

"Well...I was hoping that maybe you could make a dress for me to wear so that I can go to town with mom and dad," Flora said with a big winning smile.

"I'm sorry, Flora," Grandma said shaking her head."You need a pretty girl's dress if you want to go to town. Not a granny's dress."

"Maybe KooKoo Marta's Second Hand Store will have clothes made from fabric that we could cut and sew into a dress for you." Grandma suggested.

So Flora and Grandma went to Kookoo Marta's and searched through
all of the clothing, but found nothing that would make a pretty dress for Flora.

"I don't think that sewing a dress for you is going to be possible, Flora," Grandma
said sadly. She could see that Flora was disappointed.

"Why don't we search through my clothes closet." she suggested. "Maybe we'll
find a bright coloured dress that I don't wear anymore."

When they stepped inside the door of Grandma's bedroom
she stopped and stood looking at a pile of folded flour sacks laying on the table.

"Hmmmm...," she said. "I have an idea!"

Flora looked at her Grandmother
and then at the pile of flour sacks laying on the table.

"You're not thinking of making me a dress out of those flour sacks are you?"Flora
asked in disbelief.

"Come to the kitchen, Flora where there's more light.
When we're finished your dress, no one will be able to tell what we used for cloth,"
Grandma promised as she draped one of the flour sack squares over Flora.

"Tell me how you want your dress to look and
we'll measure and draw a pattern for you." she said excitedly.

Whatever Grandma sewed always looked
beautiful to Flora and she soon felt her excitement grow, too.

After she measured Flora's body for size,
Grandma began by drawing lines on the flour sack cloth.

Flora's job was to cut the fabric by following Grandma's lines.

As Grandma sewed, Flora looked through a box of old clothes until she found the prettiest buttons for her dress. She snipped them off and placed them in a bowl. They would be sewn down the back of the dress.

When the dress was done, Grandma asked Flora to try it on and step outside
so they could see it better in the sunlight.

The cream coloured dress was perfect!

It was the right size but was still the colour of the flour sack,
so it still looked like a flour sack to Flora.

Grandma noticed this too.

"It seems to need something else," she said.

"What if we dye it a different colour?" she asked Flora.

"How about red?" Flora suggested.

Grandma opened a container that held dried cranberries
and then dropped some in a pail of water to boil.

Once the water was a bright red colour, Grandma strained it into a wash tub and
soaked Flora's dress until it turned the right shade of red.

She then soaked the dress in cold salt water to set the dye.

As soon as the dress had dried, Flora tried it on again.
The red dress was the perfect colour but it was still a plain coloured dress.

Grandma noticed this too.

"How about ribbon?" Flora suggested.

Grandma said, "Hmmmm...I know just the person to ask. My friend Emily uses flour sack cloth to sew aprons, towels and dishclothes that she sells. Whenever Emily goes shopping, she always buys ribbons.

She may have some ribbon that you like."

Emily gladly let Flora look through all of her ribbons.
Flora picked a nice white ribbon.

"Flora?" Grandma said her name gently.
"What will you give Emily in trade for the ribbon?"

"Oh! Ummmm...," Flora said as she dug deep into her pocket.

"How about my lucky stone?" Flora asked.

"Oh my! I remember having a lucky stone when I was your age.
Thank you Flora. I will carry it with me always," Emily said.

"Wait a minute, Flora," Emily said as they turned to leave.
"I'd like to give you some barrettes for your hair.
There's a red beaded flower in the center that should match your dress."

"Why I remember my first time going to town with my parents..." she continued as
Grandma and Emily recalled the past.

As soon as they returned to Grandma's, Flora tried on her dress again
while Grandma fashioned a bow out of the ribbon.
She then sewed the bow on the front collar of Flora's dress.
They both stood back to look at the dress.

The dress was the right colour, the right size, and had a nice ribbon,
but something was still missing.

Grandma noticed it too.

"What if we sew lace around the collar and maybe down the front?" Flora suggested.

Grandma smiled. "Hmmmm...I know just the person to ask. My friend Gladys
also uses flour sack cloth to wrap around feathered pillows and cushions.

She always buys lace whenever she goes shopping
and uses it on the cushions she makes to sell."

Gladys gladly let Flora and Grandma look through all of her lace.
Flora picked a nice white fluffy lace
to go around her collar and some straight flowery lace
to be sewn down the front of her dress.

"What will you give Gladys for the lace, Flora?" Grandma asked.

"Ummmm...,"Flora said as she dug deeper into her pocket.
"How about my lucky four leaf clover?" she asked.

"Thank you Flora!" I remember having a lucky four leaf clover when I was your age.
I will press it, dry it and carry it with me always," Gladys said.

"Why I remember my first trip to town and the dress I wore..." she continued as
Grandma and Gladys recalled fond childhood memories.

When they returned home Grandma sewed the fluffy lace around the collar
and the straight lace down the front of the dress.

They both stood back to look at the dress as it hung on a chair.
It was the right colour, the right size, had a nice ribbon, and the lace was beautiful.

But something was still missing.

Grandma noticed it too.

"I think it needs some flowers,"Flora suggested.

Grandma said, "Hmmmm...I know just the person to ask.
My friend Mary also uses flour sack cloth and embroiders table cloths, doilies,
napkins and pillow cases that she sews and sells.
Whenever Mary goes shopping, she always buys embroidery thread."

Mary was happy to help Grandma and Flora with their dress
and let them pick embroidery thread from her collection.

"Flora...what will you give Mary in trade for the embroidery thread?"
Grandma asked.

"Ummmm..." Flora said as she dug deeper yet into her
pocket but her pockets were empty.

"I have nothing left to give except my pet frog, Mucky."
she said sadly as she held Mucky out to Mary.

Mary leaned back in shock.

"That's quite alright dear. You keep Mucky," she said.
"You can, however, help me with your eyes. If you visit me every day to thread my
needles that would be a wonderful way to pay for your supplies,"
Mary said as she gazed at Flora through thick lensed glasses.

On their return, Grandma sat down and began embroidering little flowers into the collar of Flora's dress.

When she was finished Grandma sighed and turned to Flora and said, "It's a perfectly beautiful dress, Flora. But I'm afraid it's missing one more thing."

"What?!" Flora asked amazed.

"It's missing **you**," she said.

"Try it on and let's take a look at you."

Flora tried her dress on and found that it fit perfectly and looked beautiful, too!

She placed the barrettes in her hair and stood looking at Grandma.

"At last! A perfect town dress!" Flora said.

"Thank you,Grandma. If you hadn't helped me, I wouldn't have this pretty dress," she said.

Flora removed a leather thong necklace with a pouch attached to the end. She opened the pouch and showed Grandma. It was filled with Flora's baby hair.

"I have one thing left that I can give in trade for the dress," she said and gave her grandmother a big hug.

"You're very welcome, Flora, and thank you for this wonderful treasure of yours. I will keep it close to me always," Grandma said.

Flora skipped home to show her mom and dad the dress
and to ask one more time if she could go to town with them.

Hearing Flora calling them, mom and dad stepped outside.
Mom was at first surprised but then looked pleased to see Flora in a dress.

"How did you get such a pretty dress, Flora?" she asked.

"Grandma sewed it for me with help from her friends," Flora said.
"So...now that I have a pretty dress, can I please got to town with you?"
Flora pleaded with both her parents.

"Well...I did say that you needed a dress" mom said. Then she looked down at Flora's
feet. "But I'm afraid those moccasins just won't do," she said laughing.
"If we can find shoes to match your dress then you can go to town with us," dad
promised. "I'll even buy the shoes," he added.

So they went to Kookoo Marta's Second Hand Store.
They searched through shelves of rubber boots, army boots,
men's and ladies' shoes and finally found a big box of children's shoes.

At the bottom of the box they found a pair of scuffed white shoes that fit Flora perfectly.

Dad paid Kookoo Marta 10 cents for them and even let Flora wear them home.

When they got home, Dad rubbed the shoes with white shoe polish.

He then buffed them with a soft cloth until they looked **shiny** and **new**.

The big day finally arrived and Flora was going to get what she wanted most
in the whole world. She was going to town for the first time,
and she had a pretty dress to wear.

As Flora's mom and dad were getting ready to leave, Kookoo Marta arrived with
her own shopping list in one hand and a little white purse in the other.

"I found a white leather jacket that was beyond repair," she said. "So...I cut a
pattern out of it and sewed this purse especially for you, Flora.
Your Grandmother told me your dress was red and that Gladys gave you red
beaded barrettes. So I beaded a red flower in the center of this purse to match
everything else you're wearing," she said as she
handed the purse to Flora along with a coin.

"Why, I remember my first time going to town.......," she said
turning to Flora's mom and dad.

"Thank you...Kookoo Marta," Flora said gratefully as she placed the purse
over her shoulder and climbed into the back seat of the car.

The trees of spruce, birch and poplar
passed by going faster and faster as the car gathered speed over the gravelled road.

Bored...yet excited, Flora dug in her dress pocket
and pulled on something wiggling to get out.

"I wonder if mom and dad will let us look at the dolls in the stores?
I'll ask my Grandma and her friends to sew me a doll
just as pretty as any doll sold in the stores!" she said proudly to Mucky
as they drove to town.

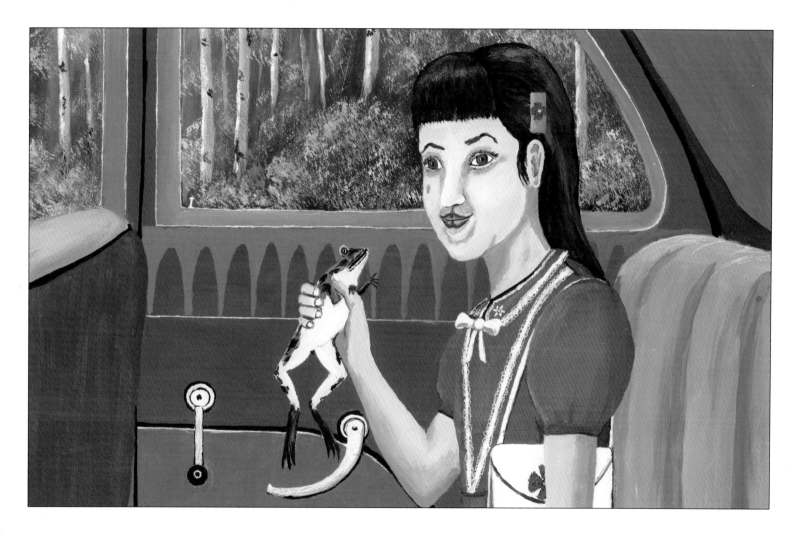

Historical note:

Many communities were remote to bigger towns and shopping centers were accessible only by gravel road. Shopping for clothing or fabric was scheduled and planned as a once a month activity. These communities did not have access to fabric and few had a used clothing store so the flour sack fabric was dyed to suit many purposes.

Companies such as Robin Hood Flour and Five Roses Flour sold their products using unbleached cotton cloth as their container. The unbleached cotton sacks were a part of Canadian family life and history. When a bag of flour, sugar, etc. was bought, families used the fabric to make various household items, e.g. pillow cases, sheets, table cloths, wash cloths, aprons, decorative pillow throws, doilies, clothing, etc. The ink that was used on the cloth was not permanent and could be washed out leaving the fabric in its original form.

This method was used to remove the ink.
1. Soak the bag overnight in cold suds, then wash thoroughly in warm soap suds.
2. If any ink remains, boil ten minutes in soap suds.